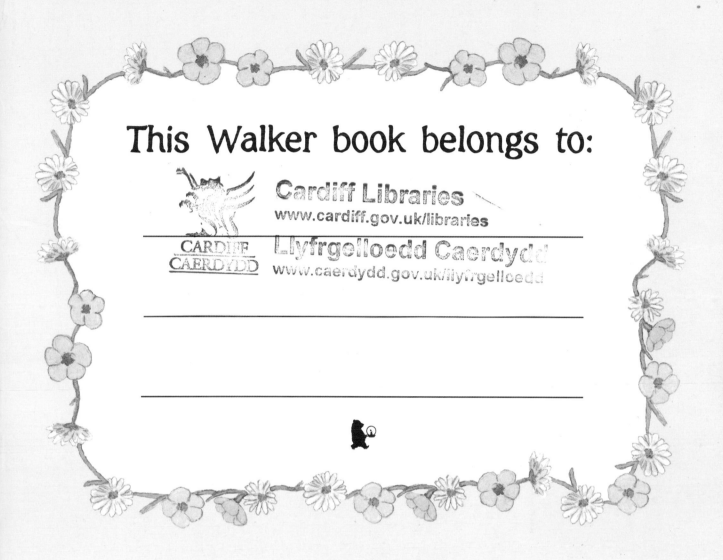

This Walker book belongs to:

For Sophie – J. E.

For Millie and George, love Auntie Vanessa – V. C.

First published 2011 by Walker Books Ltd
87 Vauxhall Walk, London SE11 5HJ

This edition published 2012

2 4 6 8 10 9 7 5 3 1

Text © 2011 Jonathan Emmett
Illustrations © 2011 Vanessa Cabban

The right of Jonathan Emmett and Vanessa Cabban to be identified as
author and illustrator respectively of this work has been asserted by them
in accordance with the Copyright, Designs and Patents Act 1988

You can find out more about Jonathan Emmett's books by
visiting his website at www.scribblestreet.co.uk

This book has been typeset in Beta Bold

Printed in China

British Library Cataloguing in Publication Data:
a catalogue record for this book is available
from the British Library

ISBN 978-1-4063-3850-8

www.walker.co.uk

WALKER BOOKS
AND SUBSIDIARIES
LONDON · BOSTON · SYDNEY · AUCKLAND

A Secret Worth Sharing

Jonathan Emmett

illustrated by

Vanessa Cabban

It was a beautiful summer day
in the woodland.
The birds were singing,
the bees were buzzing,
and the sun hung high in the sky,
like a bright golden coin.

"The perfect day to go exploring!"
decided Mole.
And he set off to see
what he could find.

Mole was not used
to being above ground
in warm weather
and so, after a while,
he had to stop
for a rest.

"Hot-diggerty!"
he puffed, sitting
down against
the side of a mossy
stump.

"Bugs and beetles!"
said a squeaky voice.
"Whatever's that?"

Mole jumped up in
surprise and found
a small furry face
peering at him through
a hole in the stump.

"Hello!" he said
nervously. "I'm Mole!
Who are you?"

"I'm Mouse!" said
the face, and gave
Mole the sweetest
smile he had
ever seen.

The stump was hollow and Mouse had a nest
inside it. It was a very nice nest,
as Mole discovered when Mouse
invited him in.

Mole decided that Mouse was very nice too,
and as he walked home that evening,
he felt very pleased with himself
for having made a new friend.
    Mole had other friends, but they all knew
        each other. Now he had a friend
            all of his own.

"Mouse is my special friend,"
he told himself. And he decided
to keep Mouse a secret and not to tell
anyone about her.

Mole had never had
a secret before. It was
very exciting and he
found it hard to think
of anything else.

So he visited Mouse
again the next day ...

and the day
after ...

and the day
after that!

Mole spent so much time with Mouse that he didn't have time for his other friends. Squirrel, Hedgehog and Rabbit all called round to see Mole, but he was never in his burrow!

"Where is he?" wondered Squirrel.

"And what's he up to?" wondered Hedgehog.

"I hope he's all right," said Rabbit.

One morning – just as Mole
was hurrying off for another secret visit
to Mouse – Rabbit, Hedgehog and Squirrel arrived.

"Hello, Mole!" said Rabbit. "We haven't seen
much of you recently, so we thought
we'd all pop round."

Mole was disappointed at first. He wanted
to see Mouse again, but he couldn't
tell his friends to go away.

However, once they got talking,
he found himself enjoying their company
as he always did.

"So, Mole," said Rabbit eventually,
"what have you been up to?"

Mole suddenly felt very embarrassed.
"I don't know what you mean," he said.
"I've only –"
But before he could finish,
he was interrupted.

"Hello, Mole! Are you down there?"
called a voice from outside.

It was Mouse!
"I thought I might come and visit
you for a change!"
she explained to Mole.

Rabbit, Hedgehog and Squirrel were very
surprised – but delighted – to meet her,
and Mouse soon made friends with all of them.
But Mole looked rather unhappy.

"What's wrong, Mole?"
asked Rabbit.

"Mouse was my special friend," said Mole glumly,
"but now I'll have to share her with everyone else!"

"But, Mole," said Mouse, giving Mole a hug,
"I'm just as much your friend as ever!
Only now I'm Rabbit's and Squirrel's
and Hedgehog's friend too!"

"Friendship is a very special thing," explained Rabbit, "but one of the things that makes it so special is that the more you share it the more you have!"

"I didn't know that," said Mole.

"So you were keeping me a secret?" smiled Mouse.

Mole blushed. "I suppose I was," he admitted.
"But now I know better.
You're a secret worth SHARING!"
beamed Mole.

Other books by
Jonathan Emmett and Vanessa Cabban